Sharing Books From Birth to Five

Welcome to Practical Parenting Books

It's never too early to introduce a child to books. It's wonderful to see your baby gazing intently at a cloth book; your toddler poring over a favourite picture; or your older child listening quietly to a story. And you're his favourite storyteller, so have fun together while you're reading — use silly voices, linger over the pictures and leave pauses for your child to join in.

Meet Jessie and Joe, their family and friends, in *Rocket To The Rescue*. They live on Little Oak Farm, a busy farm that's open to visitors. Rocket's their friendly sheepdog, but in this story she goes missing. Enjoy looking at the map together, talk about the animals and see if your child can guess what Rocket's up to! If you can, visit an open farm yourselves.

Books open doors to other worlds, so take a few minutes out of your busy day to cuddle up close and lose yourselves in a story. Your child will love it — and so will you.

Jane & Clare

Jane Kemp   Clare Walters

P.S. Look out, too, for *The Piggy Race*, the companion book in this age range, and all the other great books in the new Practical Parenting series.

AGE
3-5

First published in Great Britain by HarperCollins Publishers Ltd in 2000

3 5 7 9 8 6 4 2

ISBN: 0-00-136151-1

Text copyright © Jane Kemp and Clare Walters 2000
Illustrations copyright © Anthony Lewis 2000

Practical Parenting is published monthly by IPC Magazines Ltd. For subscription enquiries
and orders ring 01444 445555 or the credit card hotline (UK orders only) on 01622 778778.

The Practical Parenting/HarperCollins pre-school book series has been created by Jane Kemp and Clare Walters.
The Practical Parenting imprimatur is used with permission by IPC Magazines Ltd.

The authors and illustrator assert the moral right to be identified as the authors and the illustrator of the work.

A CIP catalogue for this title is available from the British Library.

The HarperCollins website address is: www.fireandwater.com

Printed in Hong Kong by Printing Express Limited

Little Oak Farm

Rocket to the Rescue

Written by Jane Kemp and Clare Walters
Illustrated by Anthony Lewis

Collins
An imprint of HarperCollinsPublishers

Jessie and her brother Joe live on Little Oak Farm. There's always lots to do because every afternoon their farm is open for visitors.

Cockadoodledoo!

One morning the noisy rooster woke Joe early.

"Look Jessie!" said Joe, "there's Dad and Rocket bringing the cows in."

Jessie was still very sleepy. "It's milking time Joe," she said, "not getting-up time. Go back to sleep."

"No way," thought Joe, "I'm much too busy."

Dad and his helper Wilf milked the cows,

while Rocket the sheepdog waited patiently outside.

"Come along Daisy! Good girl Buttercup!"

"Nearly finished," said Dad.

"Now for breakfast – I'm starving!"

"Woof!" barked Rocket.

"Isn't there a birthday party today, Mum?" asked Jessie.

"Yes, a little boy called Charlie's coming with his friends," said Mum, "so I'll have a lot to do this morning."

"Why don't you two come out with Rocket and me?" asked Dad. "We're moving the sheep into Long Field."

"Yes, PLEASE!" said Jessie and Joe.

Jessie and Joe always love being up on the hill with Dad.
Rocket was guiding the sheep into the next-door field.
"Clever dog!" said Joe.

"She's brilliant," agreed Jessie. "Those sheep always do what she wants."

Suddenly, one of the big sheep *didn't* obey Rocket and turned back into the old field.

"Look, Jessie," shouted Joe. "That naughty one's running off!"

"Quick, Rocket," they called, "don't let her escape!"

But the silly sheep couldn't fool Rocket.

The dog raced after the runaway and soon

chased her back to the rest of the flock.

As Dad, Jessie and Joe jumped and skipped back down
the hill, they heard a noisy rumbling on the road.

"It's the milk tanker!" called Joe, running ahead.

None of them noticed Rocket race back up the hill.

Woof! Woof!

BRUMM
BRUMM

Tankerman Fred collects the milk from the farm each day.

"Morning, Jessie and Joe," he said cheerfully. "Got lots

of milk for me today, then?"

"Yes, loads!" answered Joe.

Just then, Mum came over.

"Lunchtime, kids," she called. "Then we need to get the Play Barn ready for the party this afternoon."

"You having a party? Can I come?" joked Tankerman.

"Course not!" laughed Jessie and Joe, "it's just for children."

In the Play Barn, Jessie and Mum put out all the big toys.

"Look at Joe, Mum," grumbled Jessie crossly. "He's just playing."

"Come and help, Joe," said Mum. "Our birthday visitors are due any minute."

"vr**oom**!" answered Joe, whizzing by on his toy tractor.

Just then Dad popped in.

"Has anyone seen Rocket?" he asked. "I can't find her anywhere."

"We thought she was with you, Dad," said Jessie.

Dad frowned. "I thought she was with you."

Toot! Toot! A minibus drove into the car park.

"It's the birthday party children!" said Mum. "We'll have to search for Rocket while we show them round."

When the children first arrive at Little Oak Farm, Mum, Jessie and Joe always take them to Pets' Corner.

Today, Old Alfred was feeding the rabbits and he let the children stroke and hold them.

"Have you seen Rocket, Alfred?" asked Jessie.

"No, Jessie," replied Alfred.

"Who's Rocket?" asked the birthday boy, Charlie.

"Rocket's our dog," said Joe.

"She never normally runs off," added Jessie, "but today we can't find her."

"Try Bessie's stable," suggested Alfred. "Rocket loves that nice warm straw."

But Rocket wasn't in the stable.

Or with the hens.

or with the goats,

or with the ducks. "Where *is* she?" asked Jessie anxiously.

Just then Dad and Wilf arrived.

"All aboard for the Tractor Trail," called Dad. "We're off to the Top Playground."

"Hooray!" all the children shouted.

Ding-a-ling!

The children piled into the trailer, and Wilf drove slowly up the hill.

While Dad helped the children climb down, Joe
rushed ahead.

Jessie was still worried about Rocket.

Suddenly she heard a familiar bark.

"Rocket!" she gasped. "Where have you been? We've
been looking for you everywhere."

But Rocket was already bounding away.

"Look Dad," said Jessie. "She wants us to follow her."

They ran after Rocket into Long Field. A great big, woolly sheep's bottom was sticking out of the hedge!

"That sheep must have tried to wriggle through, but got her fleece caught up in the prickles," said Dad.

Baa! baa!

"It's the same naughty sheep we saw this morning!" said Jessie. "She's been trying to get back to her old field AGAIN!"

"Yes, but clever Rocket's been keeping an eye on her," said Dad. "That silly sheep never knows when to stop eating."

With a ONE... TWO... THREE... HEAVE! Dad and Wilf pulled the sheep back into the field.

"Now that's what I call being dragged through a hedge backwards," chuckled Dad, as the sheep skipped away.

Back at the farm, all the children made a huge fuss of Rocket. Dad gave her one of her favourite doggy chews as a reward.

"Good girl!" he said, ruffling her coat.

"You're a star!" said Joe.

"The best dog in the whole wide world," agreed Jessie happily.

"And this is the best birthday," said Charlie.

"Woof!" barked Rocket.

Vroom!

Lower
Playground

Tractor
Race

Car Park

Visitors'
Entrance

Ticket Office
and Gift Shop

Toilets

Herb
Garden

Café

Little Oak

Milking
Shed

Dairy

Play Barn and
Fun Room

Farmyard

Farmhouse

Pets'
Corner

Ducks'
Pond

Hen
Houses

Sharing Books From Birth to Five

Zoo Patterns
A first focus cloth book

£3.99
0 00 136130 9

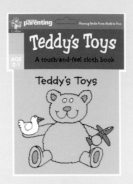

Teddy's Toys
A touch-and-feel cloth book

£3.99
0 00 136132 5

AGE 0–1

Busy Babies Go Swimming

£3.99
0 00 136139 2

Busy Babies Go to the Gym

£3.99
0 00 136137 6

AGE 1–2

TINY TRUMPET

£3.99
0 00 136147 3

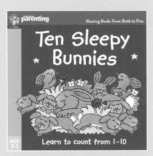

Ten Sleepy Bunnies
Learn to count from 1-10

£3.99
0 00 136171 6

AGE 2–3

Rocket to the Rescue
Meet Jessie and Joe of Little Oak Farm

£3.99
0 00 136151 1

The Piggy Race
Meet Jessie and Joe of Little Oak Farm

£3.99
0 00 136153 8

AGE 3–5

The Practical Parenting books are available from all good bookshops and can be ordered direct from HarperCollins Publishers by ringing 0141 7723200 and through the HarperCollins website: www.**fire**and**water**.com

You can also order any of these titles, with free post and packaging, from the Practical Parenting Bookshop on 01326 569339 or send your cheque or postal order together with your name and address to: Practical Parenting Bookshop, Freepost, PO Box 11, Falmouth, TR10 9EN.